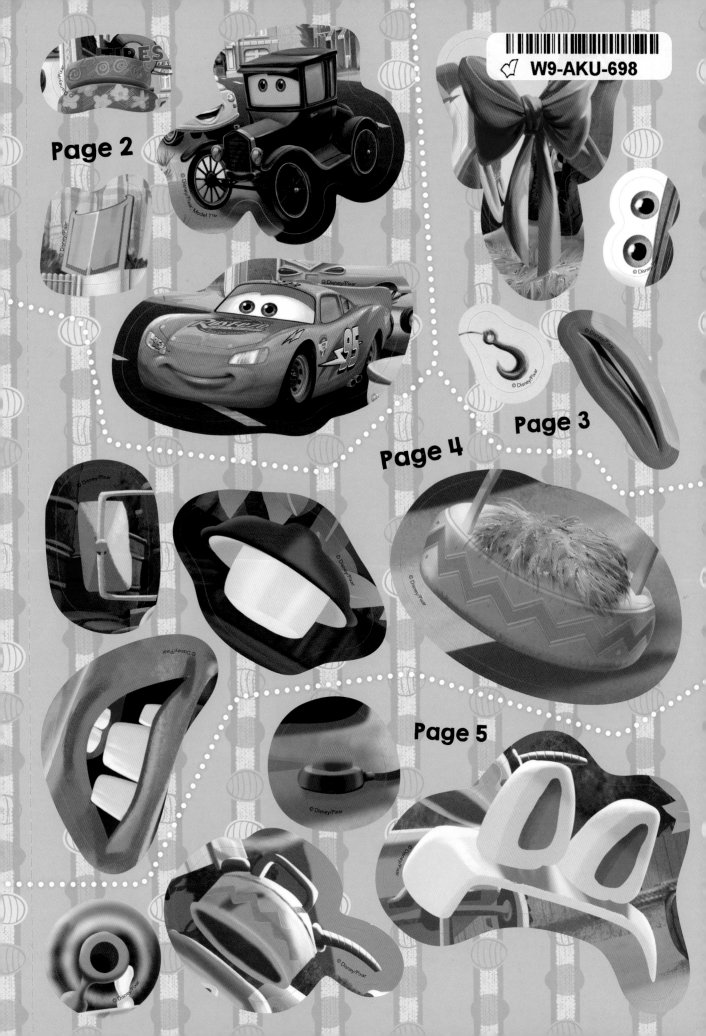

Page 2

Page 3

Page 4

Page 5

Page 6

Page 7

Page 8

Page 9

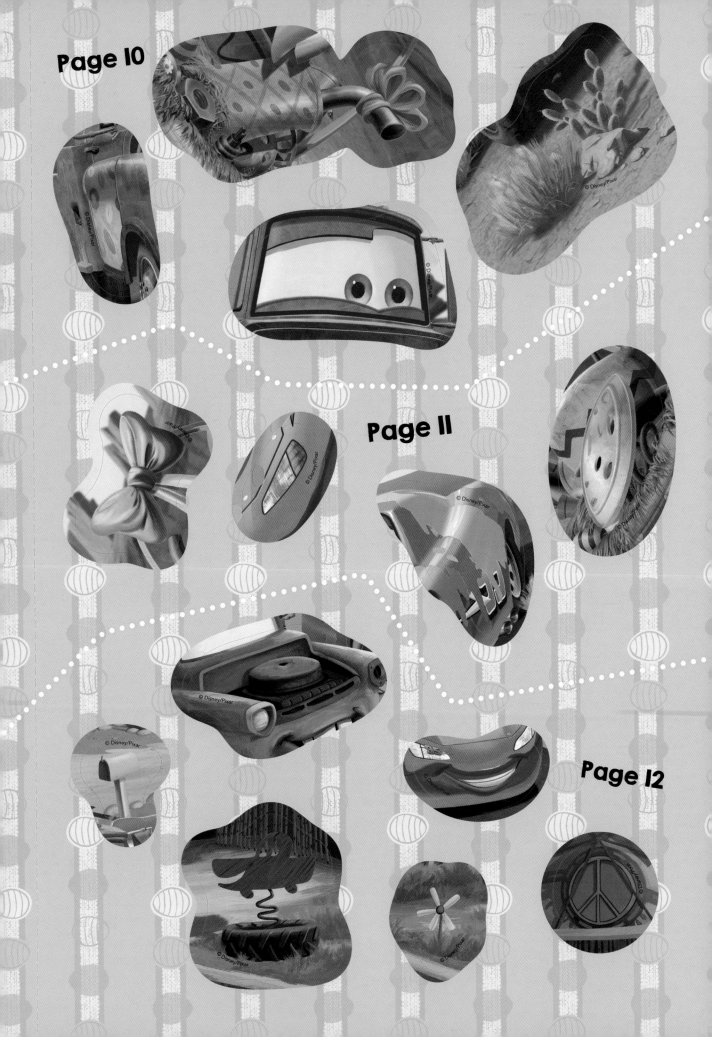

JUST FOR FUN!

Spring into Action

PaRragon

Bath · New York · Cologne · Melbourne · Delhi
Hong Kong · Shenzhen · Singapore

Easter is just around the corner, and everyone in Radiator Springs is busy getting ready for the holiday.

Complete the pictures with your stickers.

No one is more excited about Easter than Mater. "I'm going to stay up all night to see the Easter Buggy!" he tells his best friend, Lightning.
"But no one has ever seen the Easter Buggy," says Lightning. He doesn't believe in the Easter Buggy.

Complete the scene with your stickers!

Mater puts out his Easter tire, ready to be filled with Easter treats while he is asleep.

4

Lightning doesn't want his friend to be disappointed. Once Mater is asleep, Lightning sneaks over to fill the tire with treats.

But Mater has set an alarm to catch the Easter Buggy! It goes off and wakes up Mater. "Oh, it's just you!" says Mater.

Lightning decides to try again. He heads to Ramone's House of Body Art to think up a new plan. While he's there, he accidentally backs into the shelves. The paint spills all over him!

Complete the pictures with your stickers.

Mater hears the noise and drives into Ramone's. He smiles when he sees Lightning.

"The Easter Buggy gave you a new paint job!" Mater laughs, and then he has an idea. "I think I know where to find the Easter Buggy. Follow me!"

Mater leads Lightning right to the edge of town. He thinks if they wait here, they will spot the Easter Buggy leaving Radiator Springs. But soon, as the sun goes down, the two friends drift off to sleep.

Radiator Springs   Leaving so soon?

Use your stickers to complete the scene!

While they are sleeping, a pink buggy drives up to Mater's tire and fills it with Easter goodies! He leaves some for Lightning, too.

When Mater and Lightning wake up, they can't believe their eyes.
"The Easter Buggy was here!" yells Mater. "I missed him again!"

Lightning is speechless. If he didn't
fill Mater's tire with treats, who did?

FOR:
LiGHTNiNG

**Finish the
picture with
your stickers!**

24
1/4

Lighting and Mater head back into town.
"I still can't figure out who filled our Easter tires," says Lightning.
"I keep tellin' you," Mater replies, "it was the Easter Buggy."

Lightning still doesn't believe it—but he also
doesn't see the little pink buggy hiding nearby . . .

Complete
the pictures
with your
stickers!

This Super family is ready for a super Easter!

**Jack-Jack wants an Easter snack.
Draw some yummy sweet treats for him to eat.**

Speedy Dash is having an extra-super Easter egg hunt! Trace along the path as fast as you can without touching the sides. See if you can count the eggs as you go!

FINISH

How many Easter eggs did you pass along the way?

Answer: 5

16

A Super's work stops for nothing—not even Easter!

One of these pictures of Mr. Incredible is not like the rest. Can you spot the odd picture out?

A

B

C

D

Answer: D

Even in the warm spring sunshine, Frozone brings the ice!

Lightning McQueen takes the lead in the first race of the spring season.

Guido creates a new
training course in the sunshine,
throwing hay bales for
Lightning to dodge.

Warm weather means it's time for a beach race!
Race a friend to see which car will finish first.

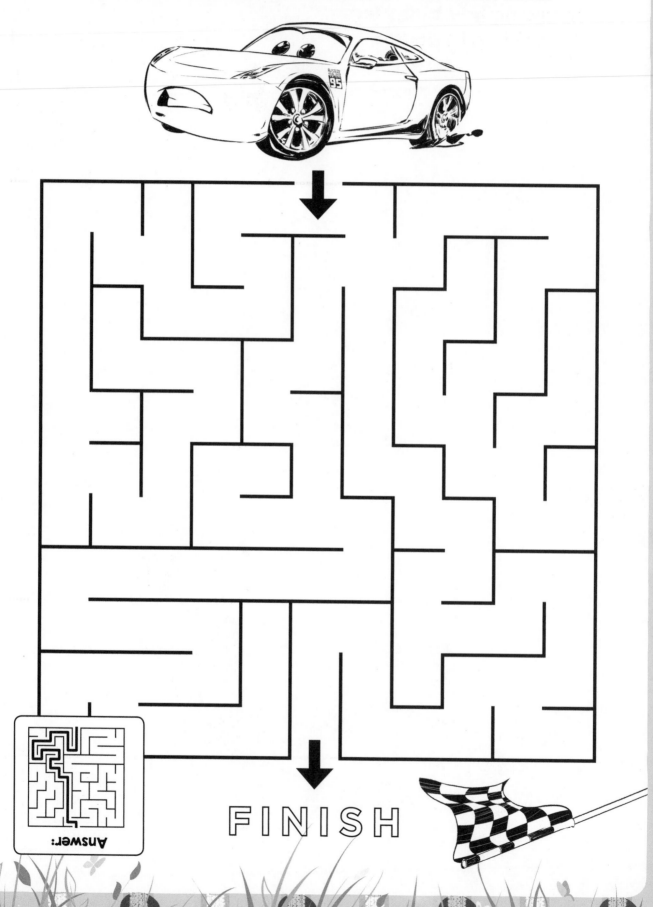

FINISH

Answer:

FINISH

Answer:

Lightning is off to race in the spring sunshine with Smokey. Color the path that will lead him to his friend.

A   B   C

24

Give your racing pals a tire bump!
Trace around your hand in the space below.

Mr. Ray takes his students to see the springtime stingray migration.

How many stingrays can you count?

I can count ◯ stingrays.

27

For Dory, springtime is about spending time with family.

Draw a picture of you and your family below.

Rex wants to draw an Easter picture for Andy.
Can you help him? Don't forget to color it in!

**The Aliens have been decorating Easter eggs.
They've made such a mess!
How many Aliens can you count?**

I can count ◯ Aliens.

**Woody has hidden lots of Easter eggs in Andy's room.
Rex can't wait to start hunting!**

Mr. Pricklepants is going to put on a springtime play for the other toys. Draw a theater around him.

Can you find all the Easter eggs hidden in Andy's room?
Color each egg as you find it.

Answer: 5

34

Can you help Woody find all the springtime words in this grid?

SUNSHINE
FLOWERS
BUNNY
EGGS
SPRING
EASTER

S	U	N	S	H	I	N	E
F	X	C	B	Q	D	P	G
L	A	K	B	M	T	C	G
O	C	I	U	K	O	R	S
W	E	Y	N	C	Y	A	P
E	Z	G	N	I	R	P	S
R	F	V	Y	W	E	D	I
S	C	R	E	T	S	A	E

Answers:

35

It's the day of the Easter Parade in Radiator Springs!

Red is watering the daffodils.

Sally loves spring showers.

Fillmore sees a colorful rainbow!

Mater has spotted some Easter treats.

**Ramone finds a new airbrush
and some paint in his tire!**

Sheriff joins the Easter Parade.

Ramone looks good with his new Easter paint job.

It's time to decorate your very own
Easter eggs! Draw lots of patterns on
the eggs below, then color them in.